Can I Tell You a Secret?

Written by Anna Kang

Illustrated by Christopher Weyant

HARPER

An Imprint of HarperCollinsPublishers

Can you *keep* a secret?
You sure?
Because I don't want anyone else to know.

Do you *promise*?

How did I keep this
a secret for so long?
Good question.

A lot of quick thinking . . .

and hard work.

It's exhausting.

And I'm very sad.
Because I really want to swim.
I'm a frog, after all!
What should I do?

What's that? You think I should tell someone?
Like my parents?
Are you sure? POSITIVE?
You wouldn't lie to me, right?

Okay, okay. I'll do it now.

Mom? Dad? I have something to tell you. I'm . . . I . . .

Why are you looking at me like that? I really AM glad they're my parents! All right, all right.... I'll tell them.

Mom? Dad? I have something important to tell you.
I... I'm...

I'm afraid of the water.

I'm so scared.
Are you sure I can do this?
Okay.
Will you stay with me?
Thanks.

Thanks for being such a great friend.
Can you come back again tomorrow?

To Emil, Lisa, and Emma, with love
—Anna & Chris

Can I Tell You a Secret?
Text copyright © 2016 by Anna Kang
Illustrations copyright © 2016 by Christopher Weyant
All rights reserved. Manufactured in China.
No part of this book may be used or reproduced in any manner whatsoever
without written permission except in the case of brief quotations embodied in
critical articles and reviews. For information address HarperCollins Children's Books,
a division of HarperCollins Publishers, 195 Broadway, New York, NY 10007.
www.harpercollinschildrens.com

ISBN 978-0-06-239684-6

The artist used watercolors and ink on 260 lb Arches paper
to create the illustrations for this book.
Typography by Rachel Zegar
16 17 18 19 20 SCP   10 9 8 7 6 5 4 3 2 1
❖
First Edition